JARMILA

ERNST WEISS

JARMILA

A Love Story from Bohemia

Translated from the German by
Rebecca Morrison and
Petra Howard-Wuerz

PUSHKIN PRESS
LONDON

English translation © Rebecca Morrison and
Petra Howard-Wuerz, 2004

Afterword © Peter Engel, 1998

First published posthumously in German as *Jarmila* in 1998
© 1998 by Ernst Weiss Erben

This edition first published in 2004 by
Pushkin Press
12 Chester Terrace
London NW1 4ND

British Library Cataloguing in Publication Data:
A catalogue record for this book is available
from the British Library

ISBN 1 901285 29 4

Cover: photograph by Brassaï *Les Fleurs 1932*
Centre Pompidou MNAM-CCI, Paris
© Estate Brassaï RMN

Frontispiece: portrait of Ernst Weiss
© The National Library of Austria Vienna

Set in 10.5 on 13.5 Baskerville
and printed in Britain
by Sherlock Printing, Bolney, West Sussex
on Legend Laid paper

I

A YEAR AGO IN AUTUMN when I was about to set off on a journey from Paris to Prague I realised in the car just before reaching the railway station that I'd left my watch at home, under my pillow. I asked the driver to stop and looked for a watchmaker's in order to buy a cheap nickel watch. There was a shop in the vicinity with handsome-looking watches for a mere thirty-five francs. I bought one and, during the rather long journey, kept an eye on its timekeeping. For the first stretch of eleven hours, it lagged a quarter of an hour behind, but then raced through the subsequent thirteen hours half an hour in advance. When we arrived in Prague though, and I compared it with the large station clock, the watch was virtually at the correct time. I walked to my hotel. I had some time and strolled down to the quay of the Vltava. A small number of muddy-brown fishing boats sail on the still, slate-coloured river. The bridges stretching over it are equipped with damming defences and are indescribably beautiful, old and new ones alike.

I was sorely tempted to hurl my watch down from one of the bridges into the river. However, I decided to hold on to it and, gesticulating to make myself understood,

entrusted it to a small watchmaker's on the left bank of
the river; the repair cost only thirty-nine crowns and I
got the watch back a few hours later in working order.
Well, working order of a sort. It now capriciously
charged forward or held back stubbornly rather like a
disobedient child who lets itself be dragged along by
excessively patient parents, tearing free from their
grasp from time to time to chase after other children
or a dog or hurtle up to the window-front of a toy shop.
The watch amused me just as children of any age, dogs
of any breed, enchant me, captivate me and make a
fool of me. For only a few francs and thirty-nine Czech
crowns this marvel of modern technology and product
of efficient mass industry had already provided me
with plenty of enjoyment.

Only I shouldn't have relied on it. Naturally, it let me
down and I missed an important appointment arranged
from Paris with a business friend at a coffee-house on
Wenceslas Square. I'd intended to purchase thirty tons
of average grade Bohemian apples from the agent and
was counting on the provision to pay off pressing debts
in Paris.

It was now late afternoon. I was sitting over my third
cup of coffee on the terrace of the café situated on the
first floor of a grand building. In front of the museum

the statue of Saint Wenceslas and his entourage of knights and magnificent horses was still bathed in warm sunlight. The slanting shafts of evening sun rested on the well-rounded haunches of one of the horses, poised in motionless splendour, its gaze fixed on the gently sloping square bustling with people.

Along the heaving road (Wenceslas Square is in fact just a very wide and elongated avenue with no real equivalent in Europe) street vendors jostled, their wares spread out on the pavement or stacked up on small wooden boards in the entrances of buildings. Travelling merchants hawked a plethora of inexpensive goods: wonderful apples (no middling wares here), frameless mirrors, tin combs, orbs of Slovakian mountain cheeses, red on the outside, honeyed within, cheap neck-ties, oranges, bananas, hand-made lace and bright peasant embroidery. It was children mostly who stopped and tried to cajole their parents into buying; from my terrace I watched well-dressed children in white gloves, tugging at the hands of their mothers or governesses, and their poorer counterparts with small, pale faces.

In a doorway directly opposite, I noticed a street hawker. Still youthful, he was no longer the youngest and his handsomely chiselled face was locked in a rather grim expression. On the ground in front of him he had placed a stripped plank of wood and on it a multitude of little toy birds were weaving in and out of one another, dancing, pecking, driven by an inner mechanism. Their staccato movements indeed reflected that of hens. Their wooden core was hidden beneath the soft, downy plumage of white, black and yellow feathers. Most of the time the trader stood there as if lost in thought but when a child came he would willingly hand over the toy to be examined, for children always want to know precisely what is going on inside their toy. When they then walked away, embarrassed at not buying, he just smiled at them. There was something odd about the fellow, almost bird-like, but far from the endearing restlessness of hens.

Every so often he righted one of the little birds that had fallen over, while never taking his eyes off the street. He was probably afraid of being arrested by the police for unlawful street trading. Frequently he pulled a little spring tucked away in the birds' feathery chest. Once again the creature struck up its spiky dance, pecking at the ground with its stuck-on beak as though there really were something to be found there. The rays of sun had long since wandered from the ample haunch of Saint Wenceslas's horse on to the swanlike curve of its neck. It didn't make any sense to wait for my business friend any longer. My new watch displayed a nonsensical hour.

When I looked up, I noticed that most of the little birds had been sold, only five or six were happily pecking away. Suddenly the man snatched them up, stuffed them into a cloth-bag where they continued to twitch, clutched the plank under his arm and broke into a run. As far as I could see there were no policemen to run from and the other illicit street vendors worked on unperturbed.

Who was the bird trader fleeing from? It surely could not be the hunched, corpulent man in a mouse-coloured coat who was wearing a dignified black bowler hat on a head showing the first signs of grey hair? He was accompanied by a pretty boy of around ten and an ash-blond, rather bitter-looking woman whose hat was rather out-dated. They were walking silently up Wenceslas Square. It seemed to me that they were wholly unaware of the profound effect their appearance had caused. Entering the park behind the museum they vanished from sight.

The street-lamps flared into life lending a magical aspect to the square. I was tired, and left. My watch ticked on. The one thing it was capable of. And I'd relied on it! I was thoroughly irate.

II

S HOULD I HAVE SUPPER? According to my watch it was only just after six. I seemed to remember it having said half past the hour the last time I checked, but that was simply impossible. No watch in the world can move both forward and back at the same time. Indignantly I sank down on one of the benches in the park behind the museum and noticed not far from me the three familiar figures. Their demeanour was still the same, grave, silent and measured. The beautiful boy (the lamps were glimmering and I could see his striking fair hair tumbling forth from his slightly overlarge cloth cap), his father, the stout, squat man, and his mother, the sullen, withered creature. The boy was alert and restless. He probably would have liked to join the other children chasing each other through the bushes on this fine autumn evening, screeching like the seagulls on the Vltava. But his parents' stern looks restrained him and forced him to pull his gloves back on and rest his hands in his lap.

I soon got up seeing as several people were waiting for me to leave my bench since it was the only one in the shadows. Two pairs of lovers raced at it, but a single man with a bundle under his arm beat them to it, the collar of his coat turned up. He seemed familiar. He had a perplexing way of looking at me, with just one eye, the other surveying the scene. This way is typical for those people whose work forces them to use only one eye, watchmakers, for example, marksmen, or doctors peering into their microscopes. That brought me back to my vexing watch. It was only when I made my way down the steps to the square that I realised it was the toy-bird trader.

I turned back for I had nothing better to do. When I passed him I saw that his eyes—his right one to be precise—were fixed on the three people. Without being seen himself he watched their every move with an indefinable expression, half hatred, half love.

I left the park. It was sultry. Rain hung in the air. Or was it the mist that rises in the evening from rivers, here as in all steep valleys? I walked down to the river through countless streets, narrow for the most part. Its banks announced themselves from afar through a closely-beaded pearl necklace of splendid candelabra lights and arc lamps. My thoughts were blank, or, rather, occupied by the toy trader with his feathered mechanical toys and by—geese.

My cursed watch had made me miss the connection with the express train in Nuremberg on my journey from Paris. The slower passenger train I had to take instead gave me the chance to become better acquainted with the Bohemian countryside. We stopped at small stations, larger villages, tiny hamlets, once even in the middle of a field.

The fields were already harvested. The woods, comprising deciduous trees (there are many birches and oaks in Bohemia, and majestic lime trees in the villages) had greatly thinned, and blackish twigs gleamed here and there through the bright foliage in the weak sun. In the bare fields, still covered in stubble, I saw gaggle upon gaggle of geese. Bohemia, surely, boasts the most beautiful geese of any country. Here they are not fed, as in France, on fish waste. In the summer they are set free on the grassy meadows, later on the fields of stubble, and come autumn they're fattened indoors in a manner both refined and cruel. Alongside the beautiful, powerful, snow-white creatures I noticed others apparently ailing, stripped of all but their large wing feathers. Their breasts, their underbellies, were naked, unkempt, reddish-grey, and they didn't march with the same cockiness and confidence as their healthy comrades; they waddled slowly, timid and fearful, and steered clear of humans, flapping their wings and starting up a furious cackling whenever they glimpsed one. I asked a fellow passenger what lay behind their strange behaviour. He didn't understand me at first, but then he smiled and replied: "You try being flayed alive, having every single hair pulled out one by one, being throttled and squeezed all the while between a pair of knees! I'd like to see you then! And the same procedure every year!" I then learned in detail how in most parts of Bohemia geese are plucked alive each year thereby producing the heavenly, light, downy feathers which made sleeping amongst the plump, snowy-white pillows of my Prague hotel such a pleasurable experience. Yet the goose not only provides feathers, but also skin, fat, meat, stomach, heart, liver and blood! Virtually every part of it is eaten. There is no escaping geese here in Bohemia.

I opted to dine somewhere else that evening, perhaps in that small, old-fashioned tavern which had caught my eye when I was following the toy trader. It was situated on Wenceslas Square beyond the statue and was bound to have simple but good fare that didn't feature geese. Most importantly, I'd noticed large glasses of almost black beer on the tables, and charmingly svelte or reassuringly sturdy blonde and brunette waitresses whose bare and firm beautifully white arms were heaving around enormous amounts of food and drink. People of modest means sat together amiably on the long wooden benches, smoking, and happily gorging on food and beer.

I stared blankly at my watch. Now it had outperformed itself. It had ground to a complete halt although the spring was tightly wound. Still furiously shaking my watch which was swishly chromed in nickel I entered the stuffy room beneath the gothic vaulted walls, suffused with tobacco smoke and odours of beer, frying and onions. I looked around. In a corner, sandwiched between two waitresses, was my friend the bird trader, his right eye winking at me and my accursed watch.

III

I SAT DOWN in an empty corner and ordered beer and Prague ham. I planned to leave the following day— but not before having sampled the ham. I couldn't make myself understood to the waitress. The toy trader, who'd been watching me the whole time with his uneven, steely-grey eyes, came to my aid; his German was not without flaws, but fluent. There was a choice of ham dishes on the menu served raw or smoked, warm or cold, with horse-radish or gherkins, cooked in wine or with noodles baked in the oven, or even as an omelette filling, with macaroni, or garnished with pickles, and so on. I wasn't really hungry and ordered without paying attention. In fact I rather would have liked to invite the toy trader to join me for a glass of beer. There were three kinds, the first a light, wheat colour, then a brown one, the last thick, heavy, and almost black. When I was young wet-nurses were given black beer like this to increase their milk flow. Was it sweet, or rather bitter like English stout? Who could I ask?

The toy trader was back in his corner, taunting the two waitresses, or groping them with his strange hands. (I couldn't say what was strange about them, and yet I've never seen anything like them.)

He took particular pleasure in grabbing their arm-
pits from behind to which they took great exception.
However the more they fended him off, the more he
would pursue them, incense them, only to turn away
with a contemptuous smile on his gaunt, manly face
which was not unattractive. One of them, a tall blonde,
very young and charming, trembled as soon as he
approached. At the last moment he turned away from
her and with a smile pulled a kind of double bird from
a small case behind him—two mechanical little birds
with feathery puffed up chests, one white, one red, that
could not and would not lay off each other. As soon as
they were placed on the polished table of ancient black
oak they started to fight as long as their springs would
let them. He gave me a furtive look, as an actor would
a critic seated in the front row, then orchestrated the
battle of his mechanical creatures, now toppling one,
now spurring the other onwards. I deliberately looked
away. I ate the thick, juicy slices of ham, *Prager Schinken
natur*, and washed it down with beer. Both were indescribably delicious. Now all I was left to wish for (apart
from a good cigar), was to drum some sense into my
damned watch.

I pulled it from my trouser pocket where I had
buried it contemptuously and picked up a table knife
which was appropriately notched and rusty. I prised
open the watch's glass cover as well as the two metal

lids. Then I took a toothpick and prodded at the balance spring, the heart of any watch as everyone knows. Everything depends on this small spring. My jab was well placed. The spring trembled, but could not be coerced into swinging once more rendering my efforts useless. Suddenly I was aware of someone looking over my shoulder.

"Not a toothpick! A steel fork, if you please," the toy trader advised, provoking my derisive response: "I'm going to clean this watch carefully, then I'll oil it a little." A bulbous oil dispenser was placed on the bare wooden table in front of me. "Then I'll shut the inner cover, then the outer one, and secure the glass lid once more. I'll turn the hands to the correct time— what time is it exactly? Then I'll go out, look for a dry spot on Wenceslas Square, place the beloved watch on the ground with the utmost of care, and—with all my one hundred and eighty pounds—will launch myself upon it."

"You and your watch will have come to the end of the road then," the toy trader remarked easily, without looking at me. The watch seemed to fascinate him. "But do allow me to take a look first, I'm from the trade."

"Ah, you, too? Just yesterday I wasted thirty-nine crowns at one of your colleague's."

"Every repair has its price, but you needn't pay me if I can't get it to work." As I shook my head and continued to jab at the innards of the watch, which to my mind deserved such punishment, he went on, as though he couldn't bear to see the clockwork suffer: "Where's the reason in this? Monsieur needn't pay me at all even if I do get it running. Agreed? Now if monsieur will just have a little patience!"

He took the watch from me with his slender, powerful hand, fetched his small case and placed it for safety's sake between his knees, as though it could go astray. A few miniature tools appeared from the depths of his shirt pocket and he secured a watchmaker's magnifying glass in one eye. The other one was transfixed in an empty stare. He set to work. He was silent, and so was I. The lovely young waitress came over every so often. The pair of us drank, peacefully and plentifully.

IV

WE SAT IN THE quietest corner of the now bustling
inn: the toy trader could work undisturbed. I
thought he would talk, I'd heard that Czech people
were loquacious on the whole. Yet either he didn't
want to or couldn't. The beer tasted better with every
glass. But it was making me heavy and drowsy, my
tongue had lost all its feeling, the vaulted room's con-
tours were obscured with smoke, everything sounded
muffled, sleepy, peaceful and still.

I suddenly jolted from my reverie. I'd heard a click-
ing noise, like the trigger of a revolver being cocked,
the noise some weapons make when the barrel is
rotated. I jumped up in fright, but the watchmaker
calmed me down. With a somewhat malicious smile
that didn't match the expression of his large, grey eyes
which in spite of everything were benevolent, even
noble, he said: "I just released the spring. The material
is coarse, but not the worst, the watch will probably
work for ever and outlive you!" I shook my head, I
found that difficult to believe. He misunderstood me:
"Don't you trust me?" he asked. "See, I trust you," he
went on, bending over the watch once more, "And I
don't even know who you are! Definitely a foreigner!"

He now picked up the simple glass salt-cellar, tipped the salt out on to the floor and placed the glass receptacle over the multitude of tiny screws and the spring that lay there gleaming blue-black, half unfurled like a tiny, inert snake.

He smiled behind his thick, silky blond moustache which glistened with drops of dark beer. I didn't want to say who I was, I never do on journeys. "Take a guess!" I said, "I've worked in many trades." And indeed, who could have predicted I was destined to become a wholesaler of second-rate apples for a French conserves factory. He picked up on my smile and responded playfully. He showed me his hands: "Now, what do you read in these?"

"Well, these tell me," I said jovially, "That you've never killed anyone."

"Oh, no, no!" he said, but, unfortunately, now I couldn't see his eyes for his right eye was glued to the watchmaker's magnifying glass and the other one was shut. "Certainly not!" he mumbled into his beard, his head bowed over the innards of my poor watch.

I could see now that he did want to talk, but still restrained himself. Instinctively he pressed his dark red, firm lips together. A quarter of an hour later he had almost entirely dismantled the watch, and all its components lay well-ordered beneath the upturned salt cellar. Putting the magnifying glass aside, he gave a satisfied sigh of a job completed and ordered some sausages and caraway rolls to accompany his sixth beer. When he finished eating he looked at me with his oblique smile, drew one of his mechanical birds from his pocket, gazed at it with that earlier look, half hatred, half love, and in one swoop ripped the bright yellow fluff from its tiny chest.

I must confess I flinched when I heard the tearing noise caused by the ripping of the little glued feathers. He kept looking at me, didn't take his eyes off me. "Let him speak!" I thought. "If only you hold back for another five minutes he will start to talk and pour out his watchmaker's heart to you." And that's indeed what happened. All through the evening (and for how long before?) he had felt an urge to open up. He had simply been holding out for the best moment to begin without burdening anybody. He could see I was waiting and so he began as though picking up an earlier conversation: "Yes, I flinched like that when, as a young man, I first saw my beloved Jarmila. There she was in front of her house, her white hand plucking feathers from the breast of a goose. Jarmila, the most beautiful in a large village full of splendid girls. Her little white feet rested on the cloth where the feathers fell, and she was stretching her toes amongst the feathers. They warmed her rosy soles, her tiny heels, and her sculpted ankles. See how it floats, how it flies! Breathe out, and

25

it is gone, breathe in, and it is there again, and all the while nothing but the stupid feathers of a silly goose."

V

" ... AND WITH BREASTS like Bohemian apples, so full of scent, and skin like down, and everything so delicate. The other women plucked geese in their musty rooms, but Jarmila's lungs were so sensitive that the tiny down feathers didn't agree with her: breathing them in caused irrepressible coughing fits until she thought she would suffocate. She clenched the thrashing goose between her firm young thighs with her skirts stretched tight and tore at it.

What can I say? We used to meet at night in a small barn to the right of the house where her husband, the old feather merchant, stored his feathers. There were no children, but she wished for them. Was that wrong? It was perfectly natural! After the crops had been harvested and as soon as the second batch of hay from his few meadows was piled high in the hay-loft her husband set off to travel the country on his cart. He was a penny-pincher. According to the villagers who laughed behind his back he even refrained from touching his young blond wife out of sheer thriftiness, not wanting to wear her out. Why should an old fool have a wife? And to think he not only had the wife for ages but, eventually, the child too. Still does, up to this very day.

Will this never change? Shall he have him forever? I often sneered at him as I lay with his wife on the heavy, rustling, soft sacks in the feather-store's gallery. She could feel the fine down feathers tickling her throat, she wanted to cough, but didn't dare to! The school-master, brother of the Oom-Pah, (I call him the Oom-Pah you know, that unwieldy brass instrument, a strident, immense kind of French horn with valves and tubes of brass, him, the old grey man for my young blond Jarmila) ... yes, that poor old scrawny school-master with steel-rimmed spectacles on his bony nose and his ears a-quiver, slinking around guarding his fat, rich brother's wife. He probably would have fancied a nibble himself, but she did not want him. Only me. That oddball, so scholarly, with all his erudite books, his hunched back, and the shiny seat of his trousers, worn-out from sitting at his desk in front of stupid kids, he did not hold any appeal. However, I was soon going to learn all about 'sitting', doing time, myself! But I am not in the least ashamed of it since I was in the right.

He hated me and maybe he was the one who betrayed us. Don't tell me, dear sir, that I was guilty of seducing poor Jarmila, stealing her from her rich hus-band, defying all law and order. It was him after all who would sit for evenings on end drinking beer in front of the local fire station with his associates, or playing for the Sunday dance with the rest of the fire brigade band, slobbering into his instrument with his fat lips, pawing its valves with his plump digits … " He bent over the cogs, screws and pins again. "The mechanism is crudely constructed," he repeated absentmindedly. "But it is not bad. Look here—there are even some rubies. It could work and it will work. I give you my word on it, and my word is worth something, although I did serve time in prison. Five years to the day, and innocent into the bargain … Five months maximum is what I should have got and my lawyer promised me that too … But, frankly, I am not a lucky man. If I fall in love with a woman, she's bound to belong to another. 'Come with me instead, we'll go to America,' I'd say. 'A relative of mine lives in the Negro quarter. He's a watchmaker like myself and all Negroes love watches. But they're both awesome and terrifying, the Negroes. Like children, they wreck them and overwind them. They have money, you can sell them a ring for far beyond its worth. It is possible to make a living there, I know it is.' But she would have none of it. 'If it were only me, I'd go with you, but now our child is on its way. Why don't you share my excitement? We'll be even happier then than we are now!' she said, pulling me close. Stifling a cough, she kissed me and instead of suffocating herself she smothered me with her white serpent arms; it felt good, and, looking back I don't regret anything! Taking my breath away she intoxicated me;

it was like a dreadful drunkenness deeper than that from dark beer; a crimson darkness fell in front of my eyes. Heat suffused each limb and turned it weak. Only my heart leapt with a furious fire and angry ardour! Surrender was sudden, and the slightest of sighs escaped, so tenderly that it barely caused the feathers to flutter, nor frightened the little mice in the corner … And I found myself agreeing with her. 'Yes,' I said, 'The Oom-Pah will certainly be better positioned to look after our child than I will having only just arrived in Harlem. But, Jarmila, have you considered that your Oom-Pah is twenty years older than you? Maybe he'll die soon. Then we'll get married, the child will be mine, and so will you! Thank God, even the rich have to die, don't they? He bought you far too cheaply for next to nothing. Just like he swindles poor farmers, paying them a trifle for their most precious down feathers. He is the mighty merchant after all. He knows all about feathers separating them into piles— the finest here, the ones of average weight and quality there, and the heaviest there … ' 'Stop talking of feathers,' she whispered, and pressed up against me once more, insatiable … "

VI

HE HAD ENTIRELY IMMERSED HIMSELF in the wretched watch and there it was, devoid of all its entrails apart from some little cogs which were apparently attached to the mechanism of the hands. He extracted one of these cogs using tweezers, held it up to the light, twirled it in his fingers, eyes half-shut.

"Here it is, dear sir! Either the cog was badly cut and was acting up for that reason or it wasn't lying dead level, thus distorting the entire mechanism of your watch. I can't say which as I don't have the appropriate tool with me: do you want to come back tomorrow evening?" I replied that come tomorrow I'd be on my way to Paris. He seemed sorry about this, but remained silent.

"Please keep the watch," I said. "You've laboured over it and I have another at home, a gold watch."

"Keep it? No, that's out of the question! Give me your address, I'll send the watch on."

"All right. I live in rue Monsieur, number nineteen. Do you want to make a note of that?"

"What for? My memory is far too good, I remember everything as though it were etched upon it as on stone. You're an educated man. Can you teach me how to forget?"

"If that's all," I said laughing, "I certainly can." Breathing heavily he stared at me with his right eye wide open. He had drunk excessively, but was still lucid. As for me, no amount of alcohol, even a quantity like that affects me.

"Well, come on! How can I forget?" he asked with unusual intensity.

I was ashamed of my big mouth. "Well, you know the answer yourself, there's only one way: old father time."

"But how long?"

"A year, or two, perhaps five."

"And if five years haven't helped, what then?" I said nothing. Nor did he. We continued to drink. The tavern was beginning to empty. The tall, slim waitress came past every now and then, skimming the head of the toy trader with her bare arm. He pretended not to notice, but his smile seemed increasingly bitter. And yet he was deeply affected as I could tell from his hands. He couldn't control them as well as the expression in his eyes.

"It's a bitter-sweet thing being the slave of a woman. And it's the same for a woman. But why should he, the Oom-Pah, the lawful husband, be entitled to only sweetness and light? I'll be honest, sometimes I beat Jarmila. Mostly Mondays. Although I danced with her nearly every Sunday in the inn as her husband was sitting on the terrace blowing into his instrument with his fat cheeks. As his musical part dictated he played only the bass notes, emitting flaccid, gurgling sounds like a merry pig: gorged and gratified, robust and rotund. His rosy, ugly mug, smug with glee, reflected in the shiny brass belly of the horn which she'd had to polish for him in the morning until it gleamed. He played well, with gusto—and downed his beers. He allowed us to dance, the young lass and lad. But he made up for it at night, taking what was his by law. Not under sacks, to the scampering of mice, not in the stinking residue of feathers, a little blood and muck always sticking to the quills ... No, upstairs in the softest of downy white quilts. I didn't take it out on him, but on her. In spite of her condition. I didn't hit her hard, mind, oh no. And she clawed at me or half-strangled me when I returned from a tête-à-tête with a girl at some house entrance or at the well. I wanted to get away from her. Enough was enough! I could easily get married: I was well-respected in the place as a qualified watchmaker and precision mechanic; not badly decorated, either, as a former artillery gunner in the war and a reservist in our Czech army. They didn't hit one another though! And when the child came, what joy for the pair of them! The pair of them! Did he deserve it? I was the one she had wanted it from, therefore it was mine, right? Tell me honestly, could I really leave it to him? It's not natural, no human could do it! And I was to be left with nothing! Did he know? Did he not know? He could not possibly believe that his wife who had been barren all along, infertile, would suddenly ripen for him, bear his fruit and bring a little Oom-Pah into the world? No, oh no. The child was mine. If there's one thing I know in this deceitful world, it's that. At first she admitted as much. It couldn't be otherwise. Just like me, as the pictures in the album at home will show you, the child was born with a halo of hair like rays of sun; his father-by-law, on the other hand, had been black as the night in his youth, and was now grey as sand. My dear sir, I don't know if you have wife and child, nor whether one should wish these earthly treasures on a man who has not embarked on this path yet … " He glanced at my bare ring finger, but I didn't respond to his question. "No," he said, "if you're not married yet, don't do it. If you have never held a new-born child in your arms and if it hasn't yet dampened your skin with its warm pee," he was chortling now, a child himself, and I could see his beautiful, sharp teeth, "then let it be. I said to her: 'Jarmila, come on, let's go now! It's the only way, Jarmila, believe me!' She acted as though she didn't understand.

'Go to Prague, you mean?' she said. 'I'd like to travel to Prague, it's meant to be so beautiful, so elegant and such fun!'

'Take our child in your arms, wrap your scarf round your head, and let's sail from Hamburg. Come on. I'll take care of you!'

'Only as far as America?' she asked in a derisive tone I didn't know her capable of. 'Off to America with a new-born baby on one arm and you, with only your good looks and wits to declare, on the other? Prague for a day, fine! America and the unknown? Never! Penniless! Forever? I think not.'

'But what's to become of the four of us?' I asked, foolishly.

'Four? Only two! You and me! Am I not yours?' she whispered, drawing me into her house, into the bed-room, showering my forearm with a hundred kisses or more, from the palm of my hand upwards to the elbow, even the place that our child had dampened. Her beautiful, full bosom heaved with every hot breath (we were of course alone in her house, her husband away buying feathers from small farmers). She un-fastened the brooch of her blouse with its splendid embroidery (the local women are all accomplished at embroidery, and Jarmila was perhaps most talented of all!); she lifted the child very gently from the cradle and held him in her hands and let him sup; whenever the strong little rascal let go of her nipple I could see it erect, gleaming rosy-red in the dusky room. I watched the baby sucking and gurgling and laughing, a picture of contentment and health, thank God! I sat very quietly, taking in everything and saying nothing. Perhaps none of this was mine. And yet I stayed! I heard footsteps outside and thought it must be one of the farm-hands, thankfully both friends of mine. Or maybe even be the brother-in-law, the schoolmaster. But she didn't think so and dropped her blouse even further: I now could see her body changed by our love, rather like dough that rises in the tepid warmth of the oven. From her navel down to her hips were slight, tender furrows, like etched lines, stretching from one side to the other. This was new to me, and frighteningly beautiful. I averted my eyes. 'Look! These are from you as well,' she said, 'They'll never disappear.' Her arms too had grown fuller and lost the slenderness of youth. 'Don't you want me anymore?' she asked. 'I love you,' I replied. It was then, I think, I confessed my love to her for the first time. But she didn't respond in kind. So I left the bedroom and the house, left even the village, and walked for an hour into a little forest. I didn't see her again for a long time. Believe it or not, I struck up a friendship with Oom-Pah's brother, the schoolmaster. He lent me beautiful books, and I made him beautiful clocks, with cuckoos or pleasant chimes. I even planned to make him a revolving globe out of a bowling ball, old maps and papier-mâché, but I didn't manage to. His sister-in-law came by often: Maruschka, a very lovely, innocent creature, willowy, and brunette, but with work-worn hands which were not as fine as Jarmila's. Her hair had a tart smell, not like Jarmila's, which smelled like corn-flowers ... My child was christened, and the Oom-Pah swaggered around proudly. He sat below at the dignitaries' table now on Sundays, while I was playing the violin on the podium, fluffing my way through. Maruschka, practically my bride, listened, and so did the other one, Jarmila. But finally the Oom-Pah couldn't bear it any longer. He came upstairs, forced me off, and took up his instrument. I just laughed. I didn't mind."

VII

"BUT WERE WE all to lead peaceful lives from now on: Jarmila, the Oom-Pah, Maruschka, the child and I? The news that the bans for Maruschka and I were to be read in church had just become known in the village, when Jarmila came to my small workshop. She'd brought a shoddy old gold watch. It was broken. She held it out to me with her white hand, but I wouldn't take it. Nor would I look into her eyes, I looked at the palm of her hand breaking out in sweat and gleaming like silver … how well I knew it, I knew every single part of her. Her poor hand trembled. I weakened and took the watch; it had been broken deliberately, the spring wound too far, the hands bent, the glass smashed. 'It would be an expensive repair job, madam,' I said, 'I don't know if it is worth it.' 'Oh, it is to me,' she said and laughed, and as I examined the watch her mouth was already at my ear and she was kissing me and weeping and laughing and whispering that I should meet her in the feather loft that evening. 'This evening?' I said, attempting to salvage a shred of pride. 'Not this evening, madam.' 'So, come when you will, but give me the usual sign and then wait for me up there until I come. Just make sure the

trap door isn't open. But even if it were, you'd tumble gently, just imagine you are falling into my arms … '
The old man had a system, you see, of separating the better, lighter down from the poor, thick quills. A hundred or so of the former would balance a particular weight on the scales, as compared to just thirty of the latter. That's all the difference there is. The first lot costs one hundred crowns whereas the others only sixty-five. I don't know whether all this sifting is worth it, but the schoolmaster thinks so and it may just be the case. In wet weather the Oom-Pah shakes one sack of feathers after another through the trap to the storage area below. The coarse, heavy feathers of inferior quality fall swiftly and settle at the bottom. The better ones float through the air for a time, and the finest, first-class feathers take the longest of all and nestle on top." He was miles away. The tavern was virtually empty now, only the blonde waitress stood nearby, the others were at the till totalling up the evening's earnings. The jangling of coins could be heard. Why was the waitress still hovering at our table although we'd long since paid? He stared at her. "Come now, Libuschka, don't fear us old bachelors! I've something to ask you!" "And what is it you want, sir?" the waitress asked in clipped, but faultless, German. "Not your love, nor your fidelity," he replied with scathing contempt. "I want to change some money, that's all." He delved into his pocket for

his day's takings: in amongst all the change was only one note, twenty crowns. Without a word, she took the money from him, counted it and went to see the cashier who was busy adding up at the back of the restaurant. The tavern was practically deserted. The tobacco smoke had dissipated somewhat, and a breeze blew in through the open windows: moist, full and pure. It must have been raining. I didn't have a watch, but it must have been long past midnight. The bank note had been left behind on the table wet with beer. He picked it up, scrutinised it, then called back the waitress. "Why did you leave the note?" he asked her accusingly as if she had committed a mortal sin. "I forgot it!" she answered shyly, but also reproachfully, for she felt embarrassed in front of me. She stretched out her work-worn, red hand. He threw the note on the ground. Quietly she bent down and picked it up. She seemed to stroke the knee of the toy trader with her beautiful, fair hair. "Hurry up, hurry up!" he said contemptuously. "So, have you finally found the note?" Once again he snatched it from her hand which was shaking impatiently for the cashier had already called her. "Why is money so dirty?" he asked, crumpling the note into a ball which he threw at Libuschka. Hurt, she shot us a furious look, aimed mostly at me as witness of her humiliation. She returned immediately with the money changed into a note and some change that the toy trader stuffed carelessly into his pocket. My poor watch was still inside out and all its parts still lay scattered under the salt cellar on the black tabletop. He pulled from his breast pocket a letter which was covered in calligraphic scrawls and tore it into little shreds which he flicked to the floor. He placed the watch and all its bits and pieces in the envelope. Libuschka now watched him calmly.

We walked out on to the square which was almost entirely deserted at this late hour. It was raining lightly. The imposing bronze horses which encircled the statue of Saint Wenceslas glistened majestically in the wet. As in the afternoon that now seemed so distant, the smooth neck of one and the haunches of another reflected the light of a street-lamp ... Cabs drove past, but the trader's glinting eyes with their hungry and pleading expression stopped me from hailing one. He desperately wanted to tell his story. The tavern's doors were locked behind us. We slowly walked across the square.

VIII

"It was around this time that my mother died. She wasn't old but in a lot of pain. The funeral left me devastated. Jarmila slipped away to see me. This time her silvery hand didn't hold any wretched watch which had been broken deliberately."—I noticed how cautiously he pronounced the word 'silvery', as though trespassing. "Instead she had come as if to comfort me! Though as it turned out I had to comfort her: she couldn't live without me, she said, the child was a constant reminder of our past. When awake she'd think of me, in sleep she'd dream of me. And I believed her because I still loved her and felt that from now on I needed to love her differently, even more, needed to love her as my mother too, and, above all, as the mother of my child! Once again we started meeting in the feather loft. Yet it was no longer the same place. The mice had vanished for Jarmila's husband had bought some cats whose green eyes startled us in the dark. An icy draught reached us from below. I wasn't sure where it came from but I assumed it was because the Oom-Pah had laid the storage room with flagstones. Admittedly it made it easier to keep the place clean … And for a while things continued like this. But

Maruschka, my bride, knew nothing of it. I would tell her to wait. I would tell her I was still saving up but I assured her she had my word. That's all she had, for I was faithful to Jarmila. One night Jarmila said to me, 'Touch my body. Can you feel how hard it is? It is not swollen yet. That won't happen until the sixth month. It's like the first time round, do you remember? But I know now my second child is on its way, and this one will be ours at last, yours. Do you understand?' Playfully she pinched my ear with her strong rough fingers but when I flinched with pain, she shuddered too and gave herself to me with a violent and increasing passion. I had never experienced her like this before, so at odds with our country girls' ways ... As she was sitting up afterwards, breathing heavily and staring with a brooding expression ahead, her hands clasped beneath her bosom, I said, 'I'll set off for Harlem, via Hamburg or Bremen. I'll wait for you there and send you money for the voyage.' She shook her head. I could clearly see her fair hair shining in the darkness of the loft. 'I won't let you!' she said. 'Why should you be hers? You're my little darling, aren't you!'—'Don't joke, and don't call me that,' I said, 'What I do is my business.' She fell silent and let go of my ear which she had grabbed again. She trembled and sobbed. 'I have to go back now, the boy is all alone and I think I can hear the creaking of a cart in the distance. It might be my husband

returning,' she said. 'Just one more month, be faithful
to me, forget about Maruschka. Four weeks, that's all!
Then we'll discuss everything!'—'But what will have
changed in just one month?' I asked her. She quickly
turned her head away as if expecting a blow. Yet I
hadn't hit her for over a year. She didn't want to answer
my question. In fact she couldn't, as there was someone calling her. She may have won the full support of
the two farm-hands, mostly due to their hatred for the
mean-fisted Oom-Pah. He rationed their food, scrimped
on wages, not to mention beer or tobacco. However, I
now realised I had to give her up to him. What can a
man do when he has got the law against him? The
next day I ran into the schoolmaster. On seeing me he
grew pale with anger, for people had started to talk
about Maruschka, his pretty sister-in-law. You know
how it is, girls never leave a man in peace, even if they
are still virgins. It bothers them more than us. More
intensely, more quietly. The schoolmaster summoned
me to the inn that evening and, coward that I was, I
turned up and swore to marry the girl. I needn't have.
But I didn't want to love so desperately any more, nor
did I want to be Jarmila's slave, nor wait for another
four weeks having already waited a month. The schoolmaster was delighted ... But do I really have to mention
what happened three nights afterwards and as often as
possible after that? All I knew was that I had a new

44

enemy: an intelligent, sober, crafty one. Soon the whole village turned against me, but also against the married couple: they did all they could to spite Jarmila. But she was proud and didn't let it get to her. She just gave a frivolous toss of her beautiful blonde hair. There wasn't much they could do to me: I was strong and the schoolmaster would have landed in a heap in the corner had he laid a finger on me. Maruschka couldn't hurt me either for she was a virgin and virgins hold no sway over men. So their easiest prey was the grey, fat old spouse, and the whole village rose to this with small-minded malice. Being more of a feather trader than a farmer he didn't have many good fields, but there was one large and lovely meadow not far from his house, and in summer its grass was mown twice. The second mowing produced especially luscious hay which was then stored in the upper reaches of the feather loft. In recent years he had needed help with the mowing and the drying: the work had become too cumbersome for him and he wanted to spare Jarmila. As anywhere else, the village needed work and money. But although he had put out word of the work three times no worker showed up. In the recent unsettled weather he couldn't get the work done quickly enough by himself, not even with the help of his two farm-hands, one of whom (the better one of course) had just been admitted to hospital. He inquired about their reasons, and while they wouldn't say: 'Listen, Oom-Pah, we won't work for you because your wife is a whore, and your second child will be a bastard too,' they still would hint at it ever so clearly ... He returned home in a blind rage. Jarmila, who normally wasn't burdened with many chores, was put to work with rake, sickle and hay-fork without delay. In the evenings I would see her just for a moment, for she was pale and tired. We exchanged a quick embrace between the house and the feather store, not far from the geese coops. We pressed together for no more than a second, yet it was wonderful for the child was alive inside her. 'Just six more weeks! You can wait, you're young!' 'Yes, I'll wait,' I said. 'I'm happy, I hope we'll be content together over there.' 'Content?' she said, finally kissing me with her warm little mouth, 'Only content? No, rapturous! Overflowing with happiness!' If only she hadn't said that! It was too beautiful, too much. I didn't trust her. I wanted to leave. 'Wait awhile,' she said, pressing up as close to me as was possible in her condition. 'Will you set off from Bremen or Hamburg? Which is it? Which is nearer? What about the cost? We have to consider everything.' But she didn't want to consider anything at all, all she wanted was me, and I shied away from her for I was afraid it might harm the child. Don't laugh, but I felt it might dirty my child. She sensed my reluctance and rebuffed me in turn. 'On your way, then!' she said, 'You'd best travel ahead to Hamburg and then straight to America, you have money enough, haven't you?' 'Yes,' I said. I'd inherited something from my poor old mother and had been saving all the while. 'Well, are you going or aren't you? When? When? When?' she asked. 'No, I won't go yet. I have to wait for it. I can't leave you on your own. Your husband might well be on to us: he is not very good to you, he is working you hard, you're made to till the fields day after day. And then ... no!' 'And when? No?!' she whispered, and so she had her way, for how could I resist ... 'No!' she uttered once more, almost imperceptibly as we took each other, I don't know quite how, but with such a burning fury, with a force as though she were tearing at me and all my blood was rushing to the surface ... How could I leave her? From then on I often waited for her, in vain. The Oom-Pah didn't let her out of his sight. The first child, my child, my Jaroslaus, was teething. He wasn't exactly unwell, but he was grumpy and wasn't drinking, whatever. I didn't get to see my beloved. He, her husband, was her daily bread, of course, lawful husband that he was.

The Oom-Pah once met me by the shrubs next to his house. He glared at me, but neither of us said a word. He made his way to the feather store; he had tools and nails with him and something else hidden between his belly and his old apron. He climbed the

47

outer staircase to the barn that I had descended ten minutes previously, but he only started hammering about a quarter of an hour later, as if on a secret mission. As it was time to store the hay in the upper loft I assumed he was nailing the trap-door shut to prevent any accident. That's how little I read his intentions. In fact I couldn't read either of them, not him nor his wife! While all this was going on I boldly took my chances and visited Jarmila. She blushed crimson, but allowed me nevertheless to kiss my child who all of a sudden refused to know me, turned pale with fright and started screaming angrily … "

IX

"I MANAGED TO calm him down. Our peace and joy, however, were to be short-lived. How could I have been so impertinent as to enjoy my child while his lawful father was busying himself in the house? I counted the minutes—the hammering in the feather loft had long since died away but I thought he'd do the rounds of the stables, feeding oats to the horses, bran to the geese and whatever else there was to do. He was back already, however, and I missed him by the skin of my teeth. I was trapped in the vicinity of the house, and had to listen to him striking my Jarmila; now he did it! I felt ashamed for doing so myself in the past! How he yelled at my child, and both man and wife quarrelled, fit to burst with anger! It was only when his brother, the schoolmaster, and his two sisters-in-law showed up that the shouting stopped. As chance had it our paths crossed again the next day. I was taken aback by his appearance. I hadn't noticed before how emaciated he'd become. He ran straight at me, hat-less, his head down low, his thick hair sticking up like an old, grey, bristly brush, trundling at me like an old buffalo that lowers its horns to charge when it encounters a younger one, running blindly. I ignored him and stepped aside.

49

It was impossible for all of us to go on living together in the village. There was hostility directed at me, too, of course, not just at the two of them. Oh, all those good Christians! It was always the same. What was heavenly manna to me? I'd been to war, after all, still half a child. Still no one would sell me a drop of milk and a morsel of bread. They couldn't refuse me out-right, but when I came to the bakery, or the farm, there was nothing left. It was impossible for me to meet Jarmila at all. A few days later we did pass one another though. She wouldn't look at me. As she walked by me she stumbled. Her heavy body nearly fell, but it wasn't me she held on to, but rather the wispy rowan tree as rich a green as ever in that sun-drenched autumn, resplendent in its dark red fruit … 'I'll be off soon, I'll do what you want and you'll have peace, all of you!' I whispered into her hot little ear. 'But I want to see you tonight, try to come, it's our last time here … Next time we'll be in Harlem with the Negroes.' I tried to laugh, but my laughter died away in my breast as she stared at me mutely. Her right cheek was swollen and I knew her husband was left-handed for he played his brass horn with his left hand. How I despised that false hand and yet, somewhere in the depths of my heart was compassion for him, even now, because his baggy peas-ant trousers hung so loose upon his gaunt frame and because we were all so unhappy. I discovered a downy

feather in my Jarmila's hair and removed it very gently.
I knew she'd been plucking geese again, it was that
time of year. Everywhere in the village women were
sitting in their sheds, the geese's warm twitching bodies
between their thighs. They plucked with gusto! Perhaps
she thought I despised her for not keeping her word as
she had frequently promised me she wouldn't pluck
the geese since the second farmhand was much better
at it anyway. But how could she have defended herself
with our child in her womb when he beat her? I
stroked her hair which was not nearly as full and soft
as when we had first kissed: 'Why didn't you come
with me then? Now the borders are closed it is much
more difficult to emigrate they say.' She wouldn't look
at me. 'I felt sorry for my husband,' she said eventually.
'I love you, but he needs me, he has no one else … ' I
wanted to be angry for she wasn't right. I had nothing
apart from her and she had lied. She did not love me
enough and had fallen for his money and the promise
of Prague's glamour. Now have a look at life here, take
a twirl in mighty Prague! Where is its splendour?
Where is the glamour of Prague? Dankness, buildings,
lanterns, rain and dirt like anywhere else. So we went
our separate ways. I had no idea whether she would
come. All she said was: 'Goodbye!' I was weak and
furious at the same time while the woman was far too
cowardly and cold. Her sweet heart was as bitter as

gall. The beautiful red berries of the rowan tree don't taste of honey either. The village offered everything apart from solace. People avoided me. There was no peace and no bread anymore for I was not allowed to make any money in my shop nor to spend it in theirs. So I went to the train station to inquire about trains to Prague and connections to Hamburg. I discussed this with the station manager who was an educated man and lived far from the village with his wife who was the daughter of a post office official from Pilsen. We were interrupted by two tramps, begging for schnapps and tobacco, an older man with shaggy hair, and a younger fair-haired one, both starving and frozen— for the nights are icy cold during this time of the year … I went to the station buffet and ordered a sausage and a glass of dark beer. Here they gave me everything, provided I paid. I ate, but it all had a bitter taste. The tramps came along, too, to warm up; I gave them something to eat, plenty of it, for money had no value for me now. They were almost falling over with hunger and fatigue. I was determined to travel. I suddenly realised that neither of the children would ever belong to me. Nor would the woman. I started to weep, I wept for all the lost years. I wept for all the reasons in the world, even for the lawful father who in his way was no less unhappy than I. For he probably guessed or even knew, thanks to his smart brother, the schoolmaster, what his wife had done to him. He was bound to this place, couldn't uproot himself. He was old. But I was young, just twenty-nine and I could easily fit my few watches and the odd bit of jewellery into my little suitcase along with my money and clothes. I didn't want to be clenched between her darling, round knees nor to hiss in wordless fury like the poor geese. I would not let her tear strips from my breast! Thus I saw myself forced to leave. But I had to see her one last time. Just see her! Why? To ask her … I had already dared a lot and even felt some respect was due to her husband for walking past me in silence and not thrashing me. Like a thief I'd entered his house many times. I had sat on his chair and she had served me his bread. Bread? I had consumed the flesh of his beautiful wife. And she didn't have a soul. She has gone to hell without a soul, or to heaven. God alone knows which.

But now I wanted to meet Jarmila one last time in the feather store. I arrived in the evening, before it was dark: I couldn't bear to be alone with my packed suitcase. I couldn't wait anymore. Nothing mattered to me. I gave the old signal—she didn't come. Placing my ear against the wooden shutters of her home below I could hear her laughing and chattering with Jaroslaus in baby talk. Why did I love her so very much? And my child even more? Couldn't I have loved only myself, or one of the farmers' daughters? Had that been possible I'd still be living there today, a happy father, a satisfied husband, and a decent citizen. A skilled watchmaker, the only one far and wide. But I just could not. I felt it was my right. A thief might steal at night. But if someone tries to cunningly or forcefully retrieve the stolen goods in daylight he puts up a fight. Of course he does! All of a sudden he clings to what is his right and so chooses his own punishment.

I called, I gave the signal, I pounded on the shutters. Only the windows on to the street had wooden shutters that closed, those on to the meadow were without. The Oom-Pah in all his bulk was leaning quietly against one of these, puffing at his pipe. A tobacco spark almost reached the spot where I was sitting in the shrubs with a wildly beating heart. The farmer smoked contentedly, his pipe hissing. His eyes rested on the tall barn he, the farmhand and Jarmila had built and which contained all the harvested hay from his lush meadows … "

X

"IT WAS PERHAPS THIS SPARK which kindled my thought. The farmer had just turned round, responding to Jarmila's call in that cooing, enticing, husky voice I knew so well. I followed a strong urge which I can neither define nor forget. I would do anything to forget for I don't want to suffer for the rest of my life. Was I seeking revenge? Or was the little fire meant to lure him away from her so that I could have her once more? At any price?

I crept to the hay-loft, and pulled out a couple of dried tufts from underneath, positioned them against the direction of the wind, added a full box of matches, and a few pages of the timetable I'd bought for the long journey. I waited for the wind to die down before setting the pile alight, nearly falling asleep in the dark. There was a strange rustling in the hay, field-mice I suspected. Somehow the place looked different. I assumed needy tenants had tried to steal hay for their thin, mangy horses, or scabby cows. How was I to know that there were people hidden in the hay, sleeping soundly—the two tramps to whom I'd been so generous in the morning. If only they had woken up! But the devil was abroad. Or God was, to punish her and me and everybody else. I wanted it to happen and then I did not. The fact was that I had taken a woman away from a repulsive old man, who'd then stolen her back from me! But to set his hay ablaze? A fire which might spread to the village? I knew it was wrong but that didn't stop me. I took a match to the hay-stack which slowly started to kindle. Only a faint glimmer moved slowly through the dark like a glowing worm. The air was damp and I thought it might fizzle out on its own ... Then I crept back to Jarmila's house. The farmer was still leaning against the window. The room was dark. They could not see me. Again the wife called for her husband, then started to sing a lullaby. Again I gave her a signal. She paused briefly, then resumed her soothing tune. But the child was a big boy! Why did she have to sing to him? If only she had remained silent, the wretched woman! The farmer tapped his pipe against the window-frame, three times. Usually he was asleep at this time. The horse whinnied, probably hungry because he had forgotten to feed it that evening. But the farmer did not move. The barn stood tall and black against early autumn's clear evening sky. A wind was picking up from there and blew in our direction ... For once in my life I'd been lucky, I thought! You've had your bit of fun, a voice inside me said, and the fire has not caught. Oh well, so be it! I wasn't aware then how long fresh hay takes to kindle."

XI

"CROUCHING, I WAITED in the bushes. Already though I was aware of a faint burning smell drifting over. Everyone in the house seemed to be asleep. The horse rubbed itself against the walls of the stable, its tail whisking restlessly against the wood. All the geese were awake in their coops and started to cackle softly. Animals sense fire and fear it. Anxiously I longed to race over to the barn, to view the fire, my fire, from close up. I knew I had to stay put, though. The reek of burning grew stronger and stronger. It constricted my chest, almost choking me and my heart beat wildly. Finally the dual tones of the fire siren sounded from the village. The farmer must have heard them as well for they were piercing. However, he took his time. I heard a mass of people rushing in the dark towards the fire and only then did the creaking front-door open slowly. The farmer stood on the threshold, and I saw her little pale hand passing him his helmet and the belt with its heavy hatchet. He was certainly taking his time. Even now! Why did I not understand? Why did we not understand? The glow of the fire was clearly visible. He must have realised long ago it was coming from his own barn, and yet he moved without any obvious urgency. First he pulled his belt too tight, then he loosened it again. I was trembling with agitation. My blood was on fire, burning more fervently than the dry hay out in the barn. He marched off at last clad in black boots and drill tunic to join the local fire-men at their assembly point by the fire-station in the main square of the village. I emerged from the bushes. I was only two steps from the door when a girl in a dark head-scarf appeared next to me and grabbed my arm. It was Maruschka. She had looked for me at my place and then run to her brother-in-law's. 'But why are you here, don't you know there's a fire?' she asked me tenderly, slipping her arm through mine. She had wanted to keep Jarmila company, and could only be dissuaded with some difficulty. Fortunately her curiosity gained the upper hand and she ran off to ogle her brother-in-law's misfortune from close up. The barn was now brightly ablaze. She dragged me along. Many women and children were now running towards the fire. I managed to lose her in the commotion and hastened back to Jarmila.

The fire seemed to gain in ferocity and sparks flew towards the village which is almost entirely thatched. However, I was concerned with only one thing and shameful though it is to admit I hungered for Jarmila as never before. I was certain of two things. Firstly, the farmer would be away for at least three hours for when a job was done the firemen always had a drink in the inn. Secondly this would be our last meeting in this country. Only a few minutes could have passed since Maruschka dragged me from the house, no more than five or six, less than ten in any case. Possessed by a dreadful premonition, I hammered on Jarmila's door and received no answer. All I could hear was the squawking of my child calling for his mother and the second farmhand trying to comfort him. I choose to call it dreadful, because both can be dreadful, anticipation of exquisite joy as well as the premonition of acute pain. The bedroom was dark, the beds piled high lit only by the glow from the fire. The flickering seeped through the window, falling on the couple's bed and the child's cot and lit up the second farmhand's long, bearded face with its simple expression. Actually older than the first farmhand but never having attained that position due to his retarded mind, he was doggedly devoted to Jarmila. His apparent simpleness hid a profound craftiness, a talent for lying, and a stubborn streak. He would confess to nothing, and swear to anything. Thus he had often rescued Jarmila and me from the jealous husband's reprisals."

XII

"I CLIMBED UP the small staircase, its wooden steps luminous in the fire's glow, and opened the door to the upper storey. I called my love's name. There was no reply. Where the unwieldy trap-door used to be, there now was nothing but a few broken paper-thin slats. A dreadful thought that she might have fallen through the skimpy planks took hold of me. How this could have happened, however, was beyond me for the bright slats which had only recently been cut were gleaming in the dark. On the other hand it was only now the barn was on fire that its glowing flames illuminated the room. Now I could even sense the fire's heat and hear its roar in the wind. A ferocious cry rose from the people outside, as if in unison. I did not understand why. I stood transfixed, spellbound. Jarmila! I called out for her once more, louder this time. I shouted as though to rouse her from an unconsciousness. I pressed my hand to my heart which beat so heavily and savagely, as it did when Jarmila tried to suffocate me in her arms.

I lay down flat on the floor and saw her immediately. She was lying below, prostrate in her white night-dress with its embroidered neck-line. She was unconscious, her arms spread-eagled, her feet naked, bare. She did not move. I was leaning over her and she looked straight up at me.

The lower storey was only about three or four metres below and usually it was piled high with feathers which created a soft mattress. Now only naked flag-stones glared at me. The feathers had been stacked in the corner in a few coarse, grey sacks which reflected the golden light of the fire. I jumped down quickly, but landed so awkwardly with my left knee on her right hand that it cracked beneath me. Not even that woke her up! I didn't feel any pain then, it was only much later that I noticed my knee was bleeding, not the left one, but the right. Jarmila's eyes were still open, one wider than the other, and looked at me with a gaze both troubled and mischievous. 'What's the matter, you little tease?' I asked, stroking her silvery little hand, warm to the touch as ever. 'For Christ's sake, Jarmila, you frightened me!' I wanted to kiss her, but something held me back.

I didn't know she was dead, but something in me must have sensed it. Her protruding stomach bulged out like a hillock. The room was now entirely lit up. I had grown accustomed to the darkness. Kneeling in front of her I could see the stretch-marks we had talked about in this very place. Now they were still, nothing moved, as if chiselled in stone. Desperately I crudely sought the beating of her heart beneath her warm, heavy breast for that is where the heart is, under the breast! Was it still beating? When I pressed my ear against her, she was still warm, warm with life. But her heart was frozen still, silent as the grave.

Outside people were shouting and running backwards and forwards between the village and the fire. I was all alone with her. 'Jarmila?' I shouted, 'Jarmila, wake up! Do you hear me? Don't scare me!' I repeated the same three sentences over and over as I tried to get to my feet. I failed. Even that was beyond me now. Not because of any pain but simply because I felt paralysed. A little down feather had blown through the barn on the sharp draught and got caught in my hair. Very gently I placed it on Jarmila's lips. It moved, it moved visibly. Was it her own dear breath or merely the draught? I touched her cool lips. Nothing. I looked at her. She looked at me. Her eyes did. Not her. I rested her head in a more comfortable position, but when I let go, her neck snapped like the spring of a broken watch. People kept running past the house and I heard someone say: ' … Jarmila … someone called Jarmila … ' I pulled myself together. I had to get help, a doctor. But there was no getting through the hole in the store's ceiling, it was far too high. So I rattled the downstairs door which was padlocked as I had noticed on my way up. The fire was slowly burning out and I was alone with the dead, in the darkness of night."

XIII

"I COULD HEAR a crowd approaching now with a cart or barrow, softly muttering. 'Put them in here,' a low croaky voice instructed. It belonged to the mayor who had only yesterday advised me to leave the village. 'Not there,' retorted Jarmila's husband, 'I don't want them in my house. They belong in the municipal building, those two.' 'It's me who gives the orders,' the mayor said. 'You'll open your barn, and everything will remain here, untouched, until the police get here.' Jarmila's husband was still reluctant: he claimed he had mislaid the keys to the padlock and would not let them break his expensive lock. It was his. 'Fine, then we'll take them to your home: they mustn't leave the premises for your house is closest to the scene of the crime. So, let's get on with it: it's the law.' Grudgingly Jarmila's husband opened the padlock. I was crouching by Jarmila's body, as if to hide her. As if there was anything to hide. But I felt embarrassed for her ... As long as I live, I'll never forget the moment before the lock broke open and they entered one by one: first the mayor, then the chief of the fire brigade, still wearing his helmet, gleaming hatchet in his belt, and holding a powerful lantern, then Jarmila's husband and finally

64

two young firemen, each one wheeling a barrow bearing a large dark mass covered by horse blankets. On crossing the high threshold one of the blankets slipped and I could see a corpse, charred, scorched, hair and nails burnt away, in terrible disarray, sooty rags hanging off the body. It was one of the tramps I'd shared lunch with that very morning. I shouted in fear for I was not in control of myself—it's only now that I am able to describe the incident without shuddering. When the farmer hauled me up from the floor and dragged me from his wife it did me more good than harm, and I had no strength to resist. 'What are you doing here? Were you planning to steal my feathers again, you filthy thief?' he asked me. 'And what have you done to my wife? Jarmila, what are you doing here? Why are you here, with him? Don't pretend to be asleep, Jarmila, get up!' He pulled Jarmila by the hand, even grabbed her hips and tried to make her sit up. The way she slumped down proved to everyone that she was no longer alive. Tears were streaming from my eyes. With his face drained of all colour, he remained silent for a long time, only stroking her hand. He shook his head. 'So he killed her. What are you waiting for? Tie him up! He's the one who broke into the storage room from above. He's the one who set fire to my barn.' I stared at the floor, neither acquiescing nor denying. I had immediately recognised the corpses on the barrows—there weren't any stretchers in the village—and was convinced of my guilt. Three people dead. I held out my wrists to be bound. There was no chain or rope though and when they tried a belt it slipped off. 'Thief, scoundrel, murderer! What, in Christ's name, have you done to my Jarmila?' This time he shouted much louder than before. By now he had gained control of himself and spotted the small pool of blood formed by the slight wound in my knee. Deliberately exaggerating his anger he shouted, 'You're not only an arsonist but a murderer too! Look at this? Do you recognise it? You killed the woman! You are all witnesses, this is blood, isn't it?' He dipped his hand in the blood and held it up for everybody to see. All stood transfixed, in deadly silence. Full of horror, I looked down at the shiny new white tiles. I noticed Jarmila's bare feet, the skin in shades of white and red. Delicate pearl-coloured feathers had been carried along by the draught and had gathered around them. This reminded me of the first time I saw her, those rosy feet embedded in light down. This sight had led to the ruin of us all.

He had lunged at me now in feigned fury, pounding and punching me brutishly, his massive knee thrust in my back like a stone. The mayor tried to protect me. Yet the farmer would not let go and pulled his hatchet from his belt to deal me a blow on the skull. 'I'll kill him. He murdered her and I see this as an act of self-defence. Such filth does not deserve to live!' The mayor threw himself between us.

'Shut up! Leave him alone!' he said. He had looked upwards and seen the broken floorboards. He continued in an even graver tone: 'You're not to touch anything else either. Your wife wasn't murdered. We are dealing with an accident. She fell on to the stone floor below. Where is the heavy trap-door you used to have here?'

'He pushed her, he murdered her! Don't you know him? He's been after her for many years. In vain. Now he has finally had his revenge.' He turned to attack me again, but my strength had returned and now I was the one to hurl him into the corner, sending him sprawling among his sacks of feathers, still clutching his ridiculous hatchet. 'No one moves until the police get here. Everyone stay where you are! Get back!' the mayor barked.

I meant to obey. He was right! Yet just at that moment the second farmhand, the retarded one, appeared. He was bewildered by all the commotion. In his arms he carried my little son who was awake and looked around with his big, blue eyes. I jumped up and ran towards him ...

Only to stop in mid-stride, stopped by the thought that he should be spared the sight of his dead mother.

A child of two years with a receptive mind should not be exposed to this sight, for he might never forget it. I snatched the horse-blanket which covered the second tramp and flung it over the half-naked young woman, over Jarmila. I never set eyes on her again. No one stopped me. We all waited in silence for the police to arrive. A few old women whispered prayers, crossing themselves, shuddering piously while deep inside revelling in their old hate. The wooden trickle of the rosary beads could be heard—perhaps this was as it should be. The lanterns had been placed on the ground, the light fell on the barrows' wheels and the dead tramp, the younger one. Jarmila's husband had gone up to his child. With fat fingers he patted his shoulders gently and tenderly until he stopped crying. No one intervened when he picked him up and carried him back to the house and put him to bed. Then he returned. He ignored me and I him. By now the old women had started to weep and the police had trouble shooing them all out of the barn. The officer compiled a brief report and announced my arrest. Jarmila's husband was also under suspicion but released on bail for he was a landowner after all and the suspicion surrounding him was not of the same gravity. They didn't believe him capable of anything, but me of everything!"

XIV

"THE BARN was cordoned off behind us. I was taken to the fire station; my hands hadn't been tied after all. I couldn't sleep. It struck me in the dead of night that I might be an arsonist, thanks to my own foolishness, but Jarmila's husband was a murderer, driven by jealousy. He had deliberately replaced the trap-door with the thin slats, he had calculatingly had the floor of the barn paved with flagstones, and he had intentionally stuffed the feathers into sacks!

And yet it had all so nearly backfired; Jarmila and at least the second child could have been mine, had I not set the fire, utter fool that I was. What could I do? Mourn the dead? Or try to avenge myself once more? Revenge is good! Revenge is better than love. Now I would not have cried, would not have held my hands to be tied.

The next morning as they were getting Oom-Pah's wagon ready to take me to the county court his brother-in-law, the schoolmaster asked smugly: 'How could an educated man do such a thing?' Later Maruschka showed up, lamenting and weeping of course, but I kept my distance. 'Don't push me away,' she said, 'You'll live to regret it!'

'What's left for me to regret?' I responded, 'I never regret.'

'I'll wait for you anyway,' she said.

'Wait? For how long?'

'Until you get out of prison, as long as it takes.'

She looked into my eyes, 'Am I not yours?'

'You're the devil's,' I spat, gripped by my insatiable fury.

'Is that your final word?' she asked, a typical woman, refusing to understand the obvious. I didn't respond for at that moment the police officer came to collect me. I pulled my cap down to hide my face and followed him closely. He took the reins himself for he liked to drive and did it well. I looked across the fields and when we passed our little wood I thought to myself that I might not walk these fields nor smell these pine needles for a long time. For it was like Maruschka had said: 'As long as it takes … ' But I still did not know the full story. How was I to know that five hard years of imprisonment lay ahead? If they had had their way they would have sentenced me to life. The old man on the other hand was guilty of the death of his wife and his second child but did not even appear before the jury. He said he had to protect himself against theft, feathers were expensive after all. A three-judge senate fined him fifty crowns for negligence, and even that had a grace period … In the village though everyone

knew who the murderer was. They didn't want him as
a fireman anymore. They didn't want him as a farmer,
nor as a feather merchant, nor as a village musician,
and he was forced to leave without delay. But not
alone! He took my son. For he was the lawful father.
And he took Maruschka, too, his brother's sister-in-law
and my bride to be. They got married just two years
into my sentence. Now she is my child's stepmother.
He is theirs according to the law. Yet he belongs to me
for I am his natural father. He is my flesh and blood.
I'd rather burn in hell with the three of them than
leave them together!"

In the meantime we had reached the hills of Vyšehrad
along the banks of the Vltava, where a road had been
cut into the cliffs with the help of explosives. Below the
rock it was sheltered and much warmer than outside.
He stopped, his breath coming fast. His hoarse whisper
resounded in my ear: "Do you think I'm a good-for-
nothing? I was in that cell for five years, busying myself
with watch-making. It was then that I came up with
my little invention, the mechanical toy. It sells well, my
child and I could easily live off it! Here, or in America.
I want him back, I'll get him. Believe me! You will see!"
"Don't you think," I said so loudly that the rock walls
reverberated, "You've brought enough unhappiness
to people?"

XV

ALTHOUGH I hadn't known the watchmaker long, I felt close to him: I recognised some of my own mistakes and shortcomings in him, although I'd never gone to such extremes. Not that I was overly proud of my restraint, it was more that I wanted him to see sense. The pretty waitress's attentions in the inn showed that people obviously still found him attractive and I thought it a waste. Some time ago, out of the blue, I was sent the watch. The glass had broken in transit, but the watch itself worked well. Unfortunately there was no letter enclosed, not a word, not even the sender's name. So the watch did not bring me any pleasure. I kept it on my desk and used it as a paper-weight. I felt ambivalent about it, and though I could not part with it nor would I wear it either although it was much more precise than the watch I'd inherited from my great-grandfather.

Just three weeks ago my concierge told me two tramps had come by looking for me, an older sort and a very handsome, very young one. They spoke in a foreign language. A strange feeling stirred in me. I was very happy. Who else could it be but the watchmaker and his Jaroslaus? Was he really his own flesh and blood, as the poor fool had believed so fervently? On the other hand I had a grim foreboding, the cause of which is obvious. I now expected their arrival anytime which led me to neglect even my business affairs. Finally they arrived, three days after their first visit. But what a change in the appearance of my friend—I almost felt moved to call him this. He was just skin and bone, his eyes hollow, his clothes dusty, his hands and face covered in dirt, every inch a tramp.

The child was the exact opposite: an enchantingly beautiful boy, large-eyed and slender, the spitting image of his father. He was a little pale, and his cheeks may have been rounder in Prague, but his clothes were clean, and his little hands, the nails neatly clipped, were white and smooth like a girl's. He was wearing a small gold ring of which he seemed overly proud. He was quite at ease and held his hand out to me as if we were old friends. I ran down to the concierge straight away to order food for both of them. The father's eyes shone longingly, but he only ate a little. The child, however, didn't lift his beautifully lashed blue eyes once, but wolfed down his meal just like any child who has not seen a well-laden table for a while. It was evening and while we were going for a walk the warm-hearted concierge prepared the guests' bedding from her own supply of pillows and sheets. The child walked proudly at his father's side, rubbing up against him like a cat. He did the same to me, and later back in the building also to the old concierge who was not known for her fondness of children but had devoted her heart to orphaned cats instead. Soon after we sent the child to bed. He obeyed without any argument. So good was his upbringing. I had rarely encountered such a charming personality which I suspect he had inherited from his mother. And yet I didn't particularly warm to him. I told myself I was getting old. Age often brings distrust. Why then did I trust the father? He was strangely taciturn. All I knew was he had crossed the Czech-German border on foot and the weather had been pleasant. What about the second border between Germany and France which was even more treacherous to cross? He looked at me innocently—as two people would who have nothing to fear from one another—and rubbed together his thumb and index finger, alluding that it had been a costly endeavour. It seemed he had entered from Luxembourg.

Why this pointless diversion? Why subject himself to another border crossing? I didn't probe. I was aware that former prison inmates often maintained connections to the criminal underworld, if only to find out about the best routes, escape points and borders, which had gained considerable significance recently. Now he lived with me and I finally knew his name, Bedřich Kohoutek. I had to remember to register him at the police commission, but he asked me to hold off for a few days. I discussed the matter with the concierge, and the good woman, usually a stickler for official regulations regarding her lodgers, was so enchanted by the cherub Jaroslaus, that she agreed to wait a few days longer. The child had soon picked up some French and could communicate far better than his father; taking advantage of the lovely weather he played outside with children of all ages in the street or the small park nearby. He always returned on time. He was so carefree, so cheerful—I never saw him looking pensive, and he never once inquired about Prague, his old father and mother. The young father and his son would often sit side by side at my table whispering. The usually reticent watchmaker would try to acquaint the child with his plans, most of which he kept from me. Why did he whisper? I did not understand his language. And I would never have betrayed him! All seemed peaceful, no police came looking, there was no mention in the Prague papers of a child-napping, at least not in the current editions.

According to the law child-napping was a crime. At this time of the American kidnappings it was considered the most despicable crime of all in popular opinion. Justifiably people were more outraged by it than by theft-induced murder. I suppose that is why my foreboding was gloomier than ever. Was it the angelic

Jaroslaus' fault? Surely he was the most innocent of us all? No angel could lock its sky-blue gaze on my eyes more innocently and directly, forcing me to look away. I took his father aside and offered him money. I advised him to escape—alone! Perhaps the man had received good news about the crossing to America that very day for he just laughed.

XVI

I WAS DELIGHTED for him knowing that he'd soon be where he had longed to be for such a long time. So I hid the fact that I'd miss him. I was concerned, however, about how the child would react to these plans and one day asked him—we understood each other reasonably well by now—whether he was glad to be going on this long voyage with Mr Kohoutek. Fetchingly the boy took my hands, pulled me down to him and whispered with sparkling eyes: "*Non Kohoutek, Papa! Papa! Papa oui*!" Followed by something incomprehensible in Czech which, judging by his gestures, meant the same thing. And how exuberantly he embraced his father when he returned home that evening, tired but happy, with one of the many necessary visas in his pocket! There was a ship leaving in three days. Crossing the border might have cost the father a lot of money, but by denying himself everything that was not strictly necessary he managed to have enough left. But a few things still had to be taken care of and while he rushed around the city to get them done the child stayed with me, playing with the stamps which he cut from my letters or playing out in the yard or in the small park. The watchmaker always returned with something for the child, fruit, sweets or a cheap toy. The boy had probably never received pocket money from him. It was therefore understandable that he showed interest in the French coins cast in nickel and bronze, some of them with an intriguing hole in the middle. I let him play with them and found it delightful that he would always return them in full. He had excellent manners and I learned from his father he was also top of his class. One would expect no less with Jarmila as the mother and Maruschka as the step-mother.

But all joking aside, when Bedřich and I were sitting together late one evening in a café and his departure was approaching, I confessed how disappointed I was in him: what about the man he used to call "Oom-Pah" and now simply referred to as "the old fellow" and of Maruschka, wilted before her time: they must be worried sick about the child back in Prague? My friend didn't fly into a rage. My concerns did not surprise him and he promised to make amends. He gave me "the old fellow's" address and asked me to send news of the child upon their arrival in America, using a typewriter and not revealing their address. It wasn't quite what I'd had in mind, but was certainly preferable to the ongoing silence which had shrouded the child's fate so far.

Was there a real solution? Could nature be reconciled with the law? From my small balcony I have a view of the park. A wooden hut stood on its periphery from where an old lady sells cheap ice-cream and coconut milk to the children playing in the park. I wanted to give the dear, sweet boy a treat, and so I handed him a franc and pointed to the wooden hut. The child understood immediately, and licked his lips with his little pink tongue like a kitten, thus indicating he would indeed use the money for ice-cream. I sat down to work and let the child go off by himself, although he tried (tentatively!) to take me with him. But I had to focus on my business and thought Jaroslaus would chatter away more freely with boys his own age than with a middle-aged man like me. When he had left, I went out on to the balcony anyway. It was really difficult not to watch him. I could see Jaroslaus gambolling with bouncing blond curls as he ran down the sloping street. He did not stop at the ice-cream shop, but continued instead at a slightly slower pace.

I wouldn't have given this another thought had Jaro not fallen ill the next day. He curled up in a ball in bed, groaning in pain, holding up his long night-gown as he ran to the toilet at least twice an hour. He ate nothing, drank nothing, and yet his cheeks and his little tongue were as rosy as ever. But why would the child hitherto obedient, and looking forward to the voyage (and to the American stamps), suddenly feign an illness? His father (who had always held children dear, but wasn't entirely sure of how to deal with them) was pale as a sheet. He insisted we call a doctor. He reproached me for giving the child money for something as dangerous as ice-cream or coconut milk, and I was relieved when the doctor said he could find nothing wrong. It must be nerves, he said, his age, and similarly meaningless phrases recited in seemingly learned tones which would earn him his fee. The next day the child was truly wretched, shivering, although he had no temperature. He scuttled out every half hour now. I did notice though that he was observing us furtively, and gave a jerk at any unusual noise at the door. And another silly detail caught my attention: when he went to the toilet, the child began to whistle, something he had never done before. While this was as insignificant as the ice-cream cone and the coconut milk, my old distrust led me to suspect that the child was lying, deceiving us, or his father at least. My instinct told me he was cleverer than we were and that we shouldn't trust him. But his father trusted him blindly, just as he had trusted the mother, the beautiful Jarmila. When I shared my thoughts with him he was furious with me, not with his beautiful, perfect child. He was understandably irritable for he had the tickets for boarding the ship which was to sail the next morning. The two small suitcases were packed. I advised him urgently now, desperately, to leave immediately, just as in years gone by he had tried to persuade Jarmila. Now, as then, it was a lost cause.

XVII

THE SHIP, the *Manhattan*, set sail without my friend and his child. I had grown very fond of him, and so I dared one last attempt. I advised him to return the child to his parents. Perhaps it was fear of the voyage, so overwhelming in the eyes of a child, that had made Jaroslaus fall ill or compelled him to play his little games. If the lawful father got the child unharmed, he might be lenient. I hoped he would then allow the natural father to see the child from time to time, to give him presents and so forth. I reminded my friend he had destroyed the old man's happiness. My friend had felt sorry for him even back in the days when he still had a wife and child. Now with his wife dead and his child gone, what was left for the poor, old, cuckolded husband but despair? None of this moved my friend. His love was unrelenting. He didn't want to share. He couldn't understand me and became even colder towards me. Once he swept the old, abandoned watch, the cause of our friendship, off my desk. Jaroslaus, polite as ever, bent down to pick it up, wiping the dust from its face, a dust-trap without the glass. His father ignored me. He was sleeping badly at night. The child was acting strangely. He refused to leave the apartment.

If it was sunny he claimed it was too hot, if there was the slightest breeze, it was too cold. His father always let him have his way. He also didn't want to leave the apartment, nor his beloved child. He had traded his tickets for a ship with a later departure date. Instead he busied himself with watch repairs that the concierge, eager-to-please, commissioned from the various lodgers in the building. His prices were very cheap and he worked very efficiently. His charming child looked over his shoulder with great interest and tried to follow everything his talented father did.

It was on one of those days when I was on my balcony that I saw a peculiar group approaching the building. Flanked by two policemen was a man who seemed familiar, but I was slow to recognise him. It was the old man, grey-haired no longer, but white, and his back even more crooked than in Prague. Yet his head with its thick white hair was thrust forward determinedly like a buffalo's. Behind him and next to a well-dressed man in civilian garb, was his wife. I ran back to the room where my friend was fully immersed in his work and shook him by the shoulder. "You've got to leave right now," I shouted at him. "The people from Prague are here. I saw them from the balcony: the old man, his wife, the police." He looked at me, his expression vacant.

"That's impossible," he said, "No one knows I am here."

"Damned fool," I cried out passionately. "What are you waiting for? Run down the stairs, past the lot of them, pull your hat low over your face, they won't recognise you, they haven't seen you since the fire, wait for me, wait for me … "—I stopped myself for I'd noticed the child, his happy eyes observing us. I whispered an address into the ear of my friend, pushing money into his hand, pressing an old hat with a wide brim over his forehead. But he didn't budge. He held tight to the table top. All my labours were in vain. There was a hammering at the door, the child darted out, opened it himself, and we heard his silvery voice, obviously beside himself with delight. Gone was the polite, muted '*Non Kohoutek, oui Papa!*' Now from deep in his chest he cried: "*Tatynek! Maminka!* Father! Mother!" The lawful parents approached the natural father. The child was clinging to the neck of his father, the old, dried-up stepmother was patting him affectionately on his back. All three were crying. My friend could still have escaped. But he stayed. Perhaps he was right to for what was his life without Jarmila and his child? And yet I would have given anything to spare him the sight of the police officer holding the card his son had written in his beautiful school-boy's script to the old man (obviously with the money I had given him for the ice cream). It gave our address and his assurance that, come what may he would wait for *Tatynek* and

Maminka and they shouldn't worry about him. And he had waited. The old man was so happy to see the child again that he said nothing to Bedřich. He didn't even look at him.

My friend was arrested. I was threatened with various charges. Supposedly I was an accomplice to kidnapping. My friend attempted to clear my name. In Czech he told the man in civilian clothes, a civil servant from the Czech consulate, that I was innocent and should be left in peace. I will never forget his look—directed not at me, nor at his child, nor at his former bride, nor at his old enemy—but at the wretched old watch. The woman took me to one side. I could see her happiness wasn't as absolute as that of the old man and Jaroslaus. Perhaps some warm feelings remained for her old love. Later I heard that she had protected my friend as far as possible. She had prevented the old man from immediately pursuing Bedřich, correctly surmising that Jaroslaus felt a strong bond to them and would return. The police, of course, had been informed straight away, but had not been given any details. All that was known was a young man had collected the child from school. What made the child go with him? Why had the child betrayed his kidnapper? He seemed so open and honest, and yet his natural father hadn't been able to read him!

The watchmaker held out his hand to me in

farewell. I squeezed it tightly and promised I would help him. I knew someone who was friends with a famous defence lawyer. For someone with a stable temperament all would not have been lost. But for him it was. I must confess that even now I did not fully understand him. He appeared to be transfixed by the watch? I gave it to him. I was able to tell the police officer that its glass was missing—and so he was allowed to take it, for even a desperate prisoner awaiting trial needs some sort of tool to sever his arteries. As for the small sharp spring inside … well, that didn't enter my thoughts.

I was given permission to see the unfortunate man's corpse. And yet was he really that unfortunate? As long as he had been a man he had known love. Perhaps it was better to die of love than of gout.

AFTERWORD

O N THE 16TH JUNE, 1940, as the German troops were invading Paris, the writer Ernst Weiss attempted to take his own life in the Hotel Trianon, rue de Vaugirard, and died in the early hours of the following day in the Hôpital Lariboisière: among the modest possessions in his small room were almost certainly several manuscripts. In all likelihood one of them would have been the next instalment of his last novel, *Der Verführer* (The Seducer), a project he had abandoned the previous year, as well as another almost finished novel banished to "the deepest drawer of my writing desk" in the spring of 1937, as he commented to Stefan Zweig. Among the unpublished texts apparently destroyed subsequent to the Ernst Weiss' suicide, including the author's diaries, was the tale of Jarmila.

Born in Brno[1] in 1882, the writer and medical doctor was only rediscovered in the sixties after a long period of oblivion: his posthumous novel *Der Augenzeuge* (The Witness) created a sensation in 1963. The title character of the work comes into contact with a psychopath named Hitler in his early days and unwittingly helps propel him on the path to power. Weiss had been part of Kafka's circle in Prague and left for Berlin in the early twenties. There, after his expressionist phase, he made his name as a writer of novels such as *Männer in der Nacht* (Men In the Night), *Boetius von Orlamünde*

1. Brno was the capital of the Czechoslovakian province of Moravia between 1918–49, and before that part of the Austro-Hungarian Empire.

and *Georg Letham*. He left the German capital at the start of 1933 after the burning of the Reichstag, returned to Prague and then from April 1934 he lived in Paris, frequently changing address.

The author would already have encountered great difficulty in placing his writings with the few remaining publishers of exile literature in those early years of emigration, but by 1937 his position was even more precarious. In a letter to Stefan Zweig with whom he corresponded for decades, he described himself as a person who "is defending both his internal and external life with dwindling strength" (19th April, 1937). He also revealed he had almost "perished due to internal bleeding" and requested that Zweig—in view of his possible demise—act as "executor of his literary will". Complaints about poor health—in 1935 Weiss was diagnosed as having a stomach ulcer—make a more frequent appearance in his letters from 1937 onwards. As do increasingly open references to his financial worries, articulated by his grateful acknowledgement of monies received from Thomas Mann, Stefan Zweig and, from the beginning of 1938, the American Guild for German Cultural Freedom.

Regardless of all his troubles, even in those dark times of exile Ernst Weiss continued to be productive and, defiant in the face of adversity, refused to give up being a writer. During this period of attempted self-assertion, he was reliant on a few close friends, Stefan Zweig in particular. He was the one, unbeknown to him, to plant the seed that became the late work *Jarmila*. In mid-October, 1936, Weiss wrote a letter to his "dear friend" as he liked to address Zweig, thanking him for the two volumes of novellas, *Kaleidoskop* (Kaleidoscope) and *Die Kette* (The Necklace) "which had brought him immense pleasure" and had "shown him that the old world we love isn't yet dead after all". He added in reference to those works by Zweig, comforting himself in a way: "Although everything now is hurtling towards the abyss with spine-chilling speed I have not lost a kind of hope and confidence".

The story of Jarmila certainly conjures up this "old world we love" depicted in Zweig's novellas: in a letter dated 16th June, 1937, Weiss told his writer-friend, who resided predominantly in London, all about it. He also informed Zweig he'd had to vacate his hotel room as the price had risen steeply, that he had moved in with friends, and that his expansive novel-in-progress, *Der Verführer* (The Seducer), was making slow progress. "In the meantime"—so his missive continues—"inspired by your volume of novellas I have written a story myself, about sixty typed pages."

It is not only out of reverence for Zweig, who was always ready to help and had been supporting him financially for quite some time, it is meant as genuine appreciation when Weiss measures his own new piece of prose against his friend's talent for the novella:

"It is the first time I recognised", so the letter goes, "what precision and subtlety and inner control this form requires and I admired you very much. May I send my piece along to you, not that there's much likelihood it can be used in any way at the moment? It's called *Jarmila* and, more or less ironically, it bears the subtitle: 'A Love Story from Bohemia'."

In the writings of Ernst Weiss that survive there is no further specific reference to this tale. Unless of course it is the "unpublished novella" mentioned by the author in a letter dated 18th August, 1939, to his erstwhile fellow countryman from Prague, F C Weisskopf, at that time an émigré in the United States. If that is the case, and it would fit the bill on several counts, then Weiss had sent his tale with its Slavic milieu to the exile magazine *The Word* published in Moscow. It was never printed there, however. At least the author received a fee for its omission which enabled him "to have ten days at the sea", he told Weisskopf.

More than sixty years after its creation, having proven true the writer's supposition that "it couldn't be used" during his period of exile, *Jarmila* is now published for the first time.[2] It certainly wasn't chance that led Weiss to the surroundings depicted in the text, surroundings he also evoked in his shorter prose works at that time such as the fragment *Sered* which is set in Prague, and in the *Messe in Roudnice* (Mass in Roudnice). As well as relating particular incidents, the author was concerned with conveying atmospheric values of that "old world we loved" as he had referred to it to Stefan Zweig: a bulwark, as it were, against the "abyss", the impending barbarism already obvious to shrewd onlookers.

2. First German publication in 1998 by Suhrkamp. This is the first English edition.

The qualities which Ernst Weiss so admired in the novellas of his friend Zweig—precision, subtlety and above all an internal unity—are also in evidence in his own story *Jarmila*. It can even be regarded as a model example of the novella genre: it has a central conflict, a tightly-executed plot, and a sharply-drawn climax and turning-point. According to particularly rigorous theory, an accomplished novella should have a "hawk", a reference to a story in Boccaccio's *Decameron*, a so-called "organizing focal point", a clearly identifiable motif or a symbol of particular pertinence.

In *Jarmila* the persistent central motif is, without doubt, the cheap nickel watch: the first person narrator purchases it in a Paris shop and its capriciousness tests him sorely in Prague but also leads to him making the acquaintance of a wretched man, the fate of whom is the main concern of the text. Again and again the broken watch crops up in the course of the story, and ultimately it is a part of the watch, the "small sharp spring" with which the unhappy "hero" of the tale takes his own life. It is not, however, with the aid of this timepiece alone that Weiss organises his novella: the story-teller works with a whole system of motifs and clues which are artfully developed and decoded one by one.

Almost as important as the watch itself is the motif of feathers that derives from it (*die Feder* in German meaning both "feather" and "spring"): the watch spring gives way to "feathers", and vice versa, and from feathers it is just a small leap to geese, and from there to other associations. The narrator contemplates the gruesome plucking of live

91

geese at the beginning of the tale, thus anticipating the situation of the watchmaker in his love-hate relationship with Jarmila as he feels squeezed between "her sweet, plump knees" like the poor animals from which she rips the down. The interweaving of associations is so deft and coherent that a circle of motifs is often rounded off and completed, when small feathers gather round the feet of the dead Jarmila, for example, the toy trader is reminded of his very first encounter with the village beauty: she was sitting on a cloth plucking geese, warming her feet in the feathers which floated to the ground.

Weiss worked plenty of clues into the framework story set between the wars. He signals the fatal outcome of the action early on, and certain warnings flare at suitable points in the text. While the watchmaker is attempting to repair the watch, the spring makes a noise "like ... a revolver being cocked", and this corresponds to a similar noise when the watchmaker—and lover—wants to more softly cushion the head of Jarmila who has plunged to her death, her neck snapping "like the spring of a broken watch". When the first-person narrator supposes to read in the expert hands of the man that "he has never killed anyone", his misinterpretation becomes a leading clue as the clockmaker only mumbles and averts his eyes—bad signs indeed. There is talk at various points of instinct and "strange" premonition which heighten the impression that the reader is witness to a fated doom.

The title character of the "love story from Bohemia" is one of those peculiar female characters often encountered in Weiss' work. He has chosen to endow her with demon-like characteristics, a desire-driven creature, who, while she is capable of kindling love and receiving it, cannot return love in the true sense of the word. This Jarmila, who almost openly parades her adultery for the whole village to see and proudly "[gives] a frivolous toss of her beautiful blonde hair", appears as a siren who draws the obedient watchmaker into the feather loft again and again with her "cooing, enticing, husky voice": that place that will be her ruin. She abandons herself to the man in a manner otherwise unknown among "country girls" and he is powerless in the face of her unrestrained ways which both attract and repel him.

The watchmaker can only defend himself verbally in his dilemma by accusing her of being "cold"—a popular idea—and shouting after her in death that she "has gone to hell without a soul, or to heaven".

When Ernst Weiss was writing *Jarmila* in his room in the Hotel d'Albret in Paris in the summer of 1937 and sending a fictitious trader of "average grade Bohemian apples" on a journey from the French capital to Prague, he would still have been able to undertake the journey through Nazi-Germany himself, had the money and motive not been lacking. Although regarded as a Jew and a writer of "decadent" works by the Third Reich, the brown-clad wielders of power couldn't simply have arrested him at the border, for at that time his Czech passport was still protection from such assault. He had made use of this two years earlier and spent some time in Berlin to receive a "free" medical examination, as he informed his correspondents.

As his "strength dwindled" the author undertook instead a journey of the imagination with his love story into Czechoslovakia, the country which had once been his home when it was part of the old Austrian empire. He transported himself back to the Bohemian countryside on a slow passenger train; he recalled the harvested fields and the battalions of geese; once again he strolled through Wenceslas Square and accompanied his hero along the river Vltava. But he also tasted the dark beer of the region and sampled the famous ham, the variations on how it is served given in a mouth-watering list that runs over several lines. In his frugal exile this would have been sweet torture, for the only thing that eased what he referred to as permanent "hunger pangs", a symptom of his stomach problems, was eating and this he could only afford to do in moderation.

The author entrusted the typing of this journey in his mind to Mona Wollheim, a German emigrant whom he had met through a mutual Paris friend. She wrote about it in a slim volume entitled *Encounter with Ernst Weiss—Paris 1936–1940* (1970). In her memoirs Mona Wollheim confuses certain things about her first commission from the writer—she would later type up his novels *Der Verführer* (The Seducer) and *Der Augenzeuge* (The Witness)—giving it the wrong title, *Irgendeine Jarmila* (Someone Called Jarmila), and muddling up the plot somewhat. But certain passages in her memoir contain interesting details. It is Mona

Wollheim who records Stefan Zweig's response to the work which Weiss had sent him—the relevant letter from Zweig had gone missing along with all the rest of Weiss' possessions. "The novella *Jarmila* is one of your strongest," Zweig purportedly commented.

Almost more significant is Mona Wollheim's indication that the author had written a second version of the story which probably only affected the ending. The existence of this version is confirmed by the *Jarmila* typescript discovered in the Czech Literature Archive in Prague-Strahov in 1995. From the fifteenth chapter onwards a typewriter is used with characters that are obviously different.

Why and when exactly Weiss reworked the ending of his Bohemian love story has as yet not been possible to verify with the materials available. There is however a notable characteristic which differentiates the original typescript from the later one. The reworking contains lead words which stand out in the text, a device which is typical of *Der Augenzeuge* (The Witness), the author's last novel. In that novel he emphasised words like "that which crushes" (*das Zermalmende*), "the base soul" (*die Unterseele*) and "the dreadful" (*das Füchterliche*) by writing them in block capitals, thus creating an atmosphere of oppressive hopelessness; in *Jarmila* the word "borders" is given the same treatment. In longhand he writes the word in capital letters and this was not on a whim, for when Weiss incorporated this change and wrote about "[questions of the] best routes, escape points and BORDERS, which had gained considerable significance recently", the subject was of burning relevance.

There is a strong case for supposing that the author reshaped the last chapter of his story in the atmosphere of the latest batch of terrible news from the Third Reich. On the 12th March, 1938, German troops marched into Austria where some of the author's relatives lived, and the next day the oppressed country was annexed by the Reich. At the beginning of October that year the Wehrmacht occupied Sudetenland, and subsequently Czechoslovakia, Weiss' homeland, was gradually crushed. That meant the corresponding borders were indeed shut to him.

While this drastic political change took its course, Weiss was sitting over his "contemporary" novel, *Der Augenzeuge* (The Witness), in which he took up a clear position against Hitler and the barbarity. One of the stylistic devices of that significant work, the visual emphasising of leading phrases, appears to have swept into *Jarmila* too, an otherwise unpolitical work. The result is a novella firmly belonging to the final creative phase of the author, and his increasingly desperate situation, shortly before he falls silent.

PETER ENGEL
Translated by Rebecca Morrison